Little Bear at BIG SCHOOL

Kathleen Allan-Meyer
Illustrated by Elaine Garvin

BJU PRESS
Greenville, South Carolina

Library of Congress Cataloging-in-Publication Data

Little Bear at Big School

Editor: Gloria Repp
Project Editor: Sarah White
Designed by Duane A. Nichols

© 1991 by Kathleen Allan-Meyer
© 2000 Bob Jones University Press
Greenville, South Carolina 29614

Printed in the United States of America

ISBN 1-57924-398-3

15   14   13   12   11   10   9   8   7   6   5   4   3   2   1

To my dear friend, Mary Connelley,
and my three little students of long ago,
Michael, Lisa, and Chris
–K. A-M.

To all my teachers . . . thank you!
And to Carol Hennessey, the best first-grade teacher
in Fayetteville, New York!
–E.G.

Little Bear hurried to finish his breakfast.

"I'm going to Big School today," he said.

"Alfred! Beartram! I'm going to Big School with you."

"You already told us," said Alfred.

Little Bear followed his brothers down the path.

"I'm going to read and write and count

just like you," he said.

At Big School, he tried to be quiet.

He looked at pictures of letters.

He counted acorns and beans and seeds.

But he didn't remember the sounds of the letters.

He didn't know the number for *three* beans.

And he forgot to be quiet.

Little Bear thought about summertime.

It was fun to go fishing.
It was fun to climb trees.
It was fun to pick berries.

But in class he could not talk to his friends.

He still couldn't read or write.

And counting was no fun at all.

One morning, Little Bear said,
"My stomach hurts."

He snuggled up to Mother Bear.
"I think I'd better stay home today."

8

Mother Bear put a paw on his head.

"You don't have a fever, Little Bear," she said.

She gave him a long look.

"But you may stay home from school today."

The next morning, Little Bear said,
"My stomach still hurts."

Mother Bear pulled him onto her lap.
"Don't you like Big School?"

"It's too hard," said Little Bear.
"And I can't read or write or count."

"Not everything in the world is fun and easy,"
Mother Bear said.
"Important things take hard work."

She smiled at him.
"*Now,* you go along to school."

Each day at school, Little Bear sat quietly.
The teacher talked, but he did not listen.

He thought about Saturday.
Maybe he would climb a very tall tree.
That was important.

Sometimes he forgot to take papers home.
He didn't think they looked very good, anyway.

Every day, Mother Bear asked,
"Do you have a paper to show me?"

But Little Bear said to himself,
"It is not important."

14

Sometimes the teacher handed out candy pumpkins to count.

The class made sets of three or four or five.

But Little Bear didn't want to count his pumpkins.

He ate them, instead.

His teacher looked sad.

She took away his candy pumpkins.

One day Little Bear said to Spunky,
"Come to the candy store with me.
I have some pennies."

At the store, Mr. Coon said,
"You need 5 pennies for candy.
You gave me only 4 pennies.
Didn't you count them?"

Another day he bumped his paw
on the way to school.
Oh! he thought. I need to rest.

He found a bench to sit on.
It felt sticky, but he didn't care.

He came into class after the bell rang.

The teacher was talking about the benches outside.

"I'm glad we are learning to read *wet*," she said.

"That's an important word."

Everyone was looking at Little Bear.

"Oh, Little Bear," she said. "What happened to you?"

Mother Bear scrubbed and scrubbed
to get the paint out of Little Bear's fur.
"I'll be glad when you learn to read," she said.

"I will too," said Little Bear.

"This is not fun," he said to himself.

"Maybe school is important.

I will work a little harder."

After that, Little Bear tied a string to his paw.

"Remember—take your papers home," he said to himself.

"Maybe Mother will like them."

After that, he listened to the teacher.

He made sets of three or four or five
with his dried berries.
And he counted them.

When the teacher nodded,
he ate them up.

23

One day he got a letter in the mail.

"It's from Eddie Squirrel," said Mother Bear.

"What does it say?" asked Little Bear.

"You read it," said Mother Bear.

Little Bear read it all.

Little Bear,

Come to my 🎈

We will eat 🍰

and 🍦🍦🍦

Go to the big 🌲

Then follow the 🚩🚩🚩🚩🚩🚩🚩

your friend,
Eddie

25

"Good for you," said Mother Bear.
"Can you count seven flags?"

"Yes, I can!" shouted Little Bear.

He ran to the tall pine tree.
Then he ran to each flag.
"1-2-3-4-5-6-7!"

26

27

Little Bear thought it was a wonderful party!

28